igloobooks

Published in 2012
by Igloo Books Ltd
Cottage Farm
Sywell
Northants
NN6 0BJ
www.igloobooks.com

LEO002 0912
2 4 6 8 10 9 7 5 3
ISBN: 978-0-85780-662-8

Printed and manufactured in China

Smelly Stories

igloobooks

This igloo book belongs to:

....

My
Super Smelly
MONSTER

SCRATCH AND
SNIFF BOOK

One day I found a monster,
hiding inside the laundry box.
He was curled up asleep,
in a pile of my smelly socks.

He had spiky, red hair,
big horns and furry skin.
And when he woke up he smiled at me
with a big, toothy grin.

I asked him what his name was,
but he just laughed and said with glee,
"I'm the grossest monster you'll ever meet,
come and play with me!"

We spent the day together,
getting muddy, stinky and smelly.
Me and my monster even made
home-made pink worm jelly!

My monster likes revolting stuff,
like furry moths and slugs.
He also loves to suck the goo
from different sorts of bugs!

But the grimy, gross, disgusting
dish my monster likes the most,
is sickeningly squiggly, wriggly maggots
spread on mouldy toast!

My monster likes to look his best,
everywhere he goes.
He bathes in slimy swamps and trims
the green claws on his toes.

Bogey
Bog

He smoothes his hair with fish oil and
cleans his teeth with mouldy goo.
Under his arms he rubs old cheese
and that smells stinky, too!

In my tree house my monster plays
all sorts of naughty tricks.
He picks big lumps of ear wax,
then licks his lips and flicks!

He loves to make big, sloppy cakes
and horrid cupcakes, too.
He covers them in mud and mould
and sometimes soft bird poo!

At my birthday party,
he put a yucky outfit on.
His waistcoat was made with snail shells
stuck together with chewing gum.

His shorts were covered with stringy slime
and crusty old cowpats.
On his hat were pink mouse tails
and flapping vampire bats!

Sometimes he gets greasy spots.
They're squishy and they're green.
When he's got a big one,
you'll know where he's been.

He loves to squeeze and squash it
and squish it, 'til it spurts.
He just loves to see how far
he can make the green pus squirt!

My monster loves a game of pretend,
we play it all the time.
We imagine we are pirates,
sailing on a sea of slime.

Our ship's flag is made from his old pants
and we wear grubby pirate vests.
We fight scary sea monsters
and use maps to find treasure chests.

My monster has got awful wind,
from eating lots of beans.
He can eat ten cans at once,
and you know what that means?

He puts on his helmet
and into his cart he hops.
He counts from one to ten,
then lets out windy pops!

My monster once rode in a hot air balloon,
up and up it soared.
But it wasn't long before my monster
got very, very bored.

He picked a fresh bogey,
loaded his catapult and pulled it back.
The bogies flew through the sky
and hit the poor birds with a thwack!

When we go away on holiday,
my monster never behaves.
Last year he got me lost
in some slimy, grimy caves.

He stomped in lots of sandcastles
and I always got the blame.
But a holiday without him
just wouldn't be the same.

I know that my monster is naughty
and never does what he's told,
and that he loves to eat smelly
mud and bird poo and mould.

But even though he's imaginary and
really just pretend,
He'll always be my super smelly,
very best friend.

Gross Monster Game

Can you find these awesome things?
They are hidden throughout this super smelly story.

Can you spot this muddy footprint?

Do you remember this clever compass?

Can you find this flying mo...

Can you find this shiny sun?

Do you remember this yucky bird?

Can you spot this smiling mouse?

Did you see this dancing cat?

Did you notice this skateboard...

The End!

Down on Mouldy Moon, in a valley made of cheese,
Alvin was playing with his jimpy-jumpy fleas.

"Come on," he said, "I'm bored of this place!"
So, Alvin and his fleas zoomed off into space.

Whizzing past the stars in his supersonic ship,
Cluster Crater was the first stop of his exciting trip.

But the fleas hopped all over the Big-footed Boos.
"Urgh, gross!" they cried. "We're not playing with you!"

At Lunar Lake, Alvin and his fleas landed with a splat,
right in the middle of a cosmic cowpat!

The One-eyed Woggles were covered, head to toe.
"Oh, dear," said the fleas, "we really need to go!"

There was a yummy picnic at their next exciting stop.
One alien asked Alvin, "Would you like some galactic pop?"

With a curly, wurly straw, Alvin took a big slurp.
But suddenly he let out the most enormous BURP!

Down a black hole they whizzed and whirled.
"Wheee!" said the fleas, as they swirled and twirled.

"Don't stop here!" said the Piggles, with a scowl.
"The pong from your ship is simply foul!"

"Mmm," said Alvin, "I can smell something yummy.
Let's land at Crunchy Comet and eat something scrummy."

But too many buns made his big tummy grumble.
Then his bottom did a burp that made the ground rumble!

Bursting with pretty perfumes galore,
the next place made Alvin feel worse than before.

The Pufflings covered him in sweet-smelling sprays.
Running off he cried, "I won't smell stinky for days!"

Twisting and turning, they landed safely on the ground.
In Twilight Town, stardust was falling all around.

The dust made Alvin's nose tickle. Suddenly he went, "Ah-choo!"
He covered the Long-nosed Noodles in green galactic goo!

At Cosmic Creek, the Fibbles were playing in the sun.
"Can I join in, too?" said Alvin. "We'll have lots of fun."

"Let's play," he said, throwing stinky space pies.
"We don't like smelly stuff, Alvin!" the aliens cried.

At Meteor Meadow, the Polettes held their little noses,
as Alvin's super stench killed their daisies and roses.

The aliens shouted, "Take your fleas and go away!
You smell gross. We don't want to play today."

Alvin and his fleas were far from home.
They had made no friends and were all alone.

With tears in his eyes, Alvin took a big sniff,
when he smelled the most delicious whiff!

"This is Planet Pong," the Stinky Snoggles said with glee.
"We'll play with you and your jimpy-jumpy fleas!"

With lots of gross smells, stinks, goo and slime,
Alvin and his fleas had the most wonderful time!

Alvin the Alien's Awesome Activity

Can you find these amazing things?
They are hidden throughout this awesome alien story.

Can you find this 1-eyed cow?

Do you remember these cute Piggles?

Did you see this yummy ice-cream?

Can you find this 3-eyed fish?

Did you notice this jar of eyeballs?

Can you spot this stinky space pie?

Where was this blue alien?

Can you spot this alien spaceship?

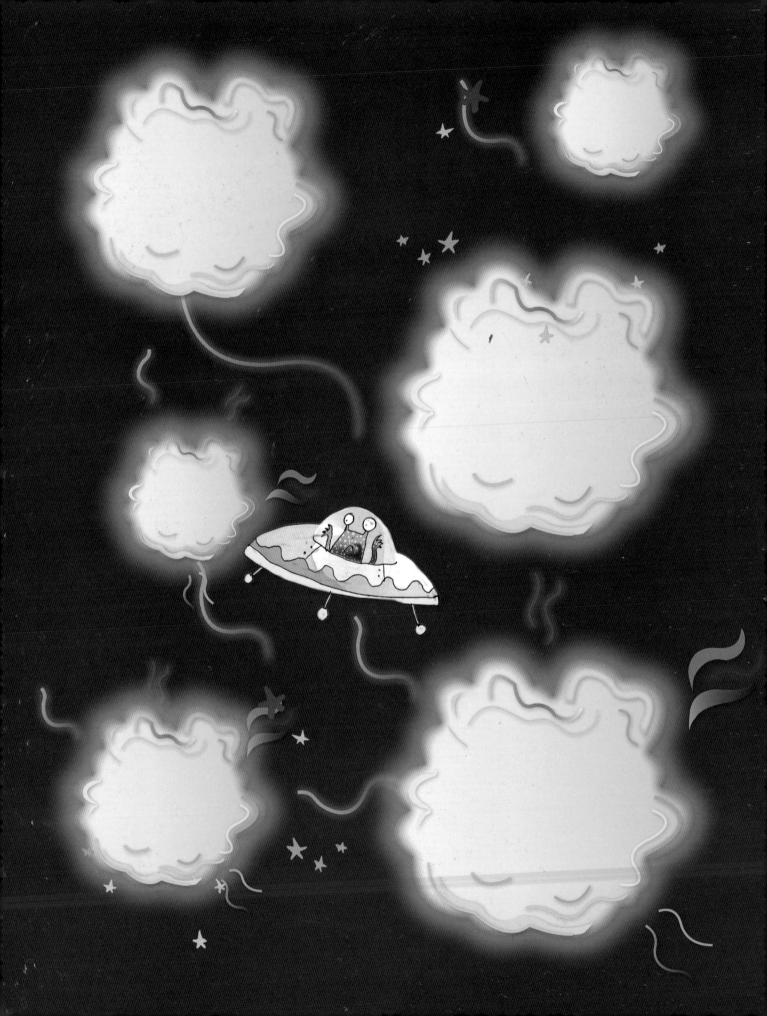